FIFE COUNCIL LIBRARIES

FB106596

KT-425-816

Polly and the Pirates

Tony Bradman

Illustrated by James Davies

FIFE COUNCIL	
106596	
PETERS	02-Sep-2013
JF	£4.99
JICR	KY

J. D.

EGMONT
We bring stories to life

Book Band: Gold

This edition first published in Great Britain 2013
by Egmont UK Ltd
The Yellow Building, 1 Nicholas Road, London W11 4AN
Text copyright © Tony Bradman 2013
Illustrations copyright © James Davies 2013
The author and illustrator have asserted their moral rights.
ISBN 978 1 4052 6412 9
10 9 8 7 6 5 4 3 2 1
www.egmont.co.uk
A CIP catalogue record for this title is available from the British Library.
Printed in Singapore.
52576/1
All rights reserved. No part of this publication may be reproduced,
stored in a retrieval system, or transmitted, in any form or by any means,
electronic, mechanical, photocopying, recording or otherwise, without the
prior permission of the publisher and copyright owner.
Stay safe online. Egmont is not responsible for content hosted by third parties.

EGMONT LUCKY COIN

Our story began over a century ago, when seventeen-year-old Egmont Harald Petersen found a coin in the street.

He was on his way to buy a flyswatter, a small hand-operated printing machine that he then set up in his tiny apartment.

The coin brought him such good luck that today Egmont has offices in over 30 countries around the world. And that lucky coin is still kept at the company's head offices in Denmark.

CONTENTS

Red Bananas

Cast Adrift!

It was a cold and blustery day out on the ocean waves, and *The Jolly Herbert*'s sails flapped and snapped in the wind. But the pirates weren't taking any notice of the weather. For something far more interesting was happening . . .

Bad Bart stood on the poop deck, scowling down at Cap'n Caleb and his wife Keel-Haul Annie. The couple were surrounded by the ship's crew – the ugliest, scurviest, meanest bunch of buccaneers you ever did see, each one armed to the teeth. Annie was holding a small bundle in her arms, and scowled back.

'We'll give 'ee one last chance to end this mutiny, Bart,' Annie said.

'Aye, fair's fair,' said Caleb. 'No hard feelings if ye give in now.'

'No hard feelings? It's too late for that,' growled Bad Bart. 'The pair of 'ee should have thought how we might feel about the terrible things ye've done.'

The crew muttered and grumbled and shook their cutlasses in agreement.

'Stop talkin' bilge!' said Caleb. 'We've always been good skippers.'

'Ye were,' said Bad Bart. 'Until the day ye decided . . . *to get married.*'

'Aye, we'll never forgive 'ee for makin' us wear them there page-boy outfits,' hissed one of the men. 'And as for those hats and shoes . . . Ha!'

'Well ye didn't complain at the time,' said Annie. 'Not that ye'd have dared.'

'We might have if we'd known what horrors were to come,' growled Bad Bart. 'For after that ye did the worst thing of all. *Ye had a baby!*'

Just then a loud wailing came from Annie's bundle.

'And what a lovely baby our Polly is,' said Annie. She and Caleb beamed at their daughter.

'We don't think so,' said Bad Bart. 'She keeps us awake all night with her blasted cryin', and those nappies of hers stink even more than we do!'

'How would ye know?' said Caleb. 'Ye've never offered to change one.'

'Shiver me timbers,' groaned Bad Bart. 'We're not nursemaids, we're PIRATES! Anyhow, enough of this talkin'. I'd like to make 'ee walk the plank, but I'll settle for gettin' rid of 'ee without any fun. Put 'em in the dinghy, lads!'

The crew pushed Caleb and Annie to the

side of the ship. Caleb climbed down to the dinghy. Annie lowered Polly, then climbed down herself.

'This ain't over between us, Bart,' said Annie. 'Just ye wait and see.'

'I won't hold me breath,' laughed Bad Bart. 'Right . . . cast 'em adrift!'

The Jolly Herbert sailed on, leaving the dinghy in its wake.

Settling Down

Things looked grim for the little family. They didn't have much food and water, and they were a long way from the nearest land. But Caleb and Annie had been at sea all their lives, so they soon managed to rig a sail and set a course.

One day went past, then another. Polly gurgled away and seemed happy, and that kept her parents going. They ate the fish they caught . . . and they talked.

'I hates to say it,' muttered Caleb, 'but maybe Bart's done us a favour.'

'Ye must be jokin'!' spluttered Annie. 'Has the sun boiled your brains?'

'Think about it, my love. A pirate ship ain't really a place for a baby.'

'Ye be dead right there, Caleb,' Annie sighed. 'But what shall we do, then? Bein' pirates be the only way we know how to make a proper livin'.'

'Well, we'll have to think of somethin' else. For our Polly's sake . . .'

Just then a dark cloud covered the sun and the wind whipped up a terrible storm. The waves were like mountains, and the little dinghy was nearly swamped.

But they kept going through the night, and in the morning the sea was calmer. Caleb peered at the distant horizon. '*Land ho!*' he yelled, and they cheered.

It took them quite a while to settle down ashore. They found a house a long way inland and made it, er . . . comfortable . . .

Annie got a job handing out parking tickets (nobody ever argued with her) . . .

. . . and Caleb stayed at home to take care of Polly.

Polly grew, of course.
She learned to crawl . . .
and walk . . .

SQUAWWK!

. . . and before long
she was running . . .
and jumping . . .
and climbing. She
learned to talk as well.

'Steady as she goes!' she would say.
Or, 'Blisterin' barnacles!' Or, 'Easy on
the cornflakes, Pa, I've had my fill!' Or,
'Hooray and up she rises!' in the bath.

'Ah, what a wonderful daughter we have,'
said Caleb one day. He and Annie were sitting
in the park, watching Polly enjoy herself on
the swings.

'Aye, things have turned out fine,' said
Annie. Then she sighed. 'Still, I'll admit to
feeling a mite bored sometimes. I do sorely
miss the pirate life.'

'Me too,' said Caleb, sighing himself. 'But Polly be fine, and that be all that do count. Look lively there, Polly – boarders on your starboard bow!'

Things never stay the same, though. Polly kept growing, of course.

Soon it was time for her to go to school . . .

Parents' Evening

Polly's teacher was called Miss Primly, and
Polly thought she was wonderful. In fact,
as far as Polly was concerned, Miss Primly
could do no wrong. Caleb and Annie quickly
got used to hearing Miss Primly's nuggets of
wisdom.

'Miss Primly says you should start the day
with a good breakfast,' said Polly. ('Couldn't
agree more!' said Caleb.) Or: 'Miss Primly
says a tidy house is the sign of a tidy mind.'
('I do like things to be shipshape meself,' said
Annie.)

'Ah, she do seem a proper nice lady, does this Miss Primly,' said Caleb.

'Aye, so she do,' said Annie. 'I hope we gets the chance to meet her.'

'Your wish is granted, Ma!' said Polly. 'It's Parents' Evening tonight . . .'

The school was crowded when they got there, and they had to wait a while.

Some of the other parents stared at Caleb and Annie. Annie stared right back.

'It's good to meet you,' said Miss Primly. 'Polly is such a lovely girl.'

'It's kind of 'ee to say so,' said Caleb. 'But we did know that already.'

He beamed happily at Annie, and they both beamed at Miss Primly.

'Although I have to say she can sometimes be a bit loud,' said Miss Primly. 'And she does have . . . how shall I put this? An interesting turn of phrase.'

'Perishin' parrots!' said Caleb. 'Can't say I've noticed that meself.'

'We wondered how she was gettin' on with her studies,' said Annie.

Perishin' parrots!

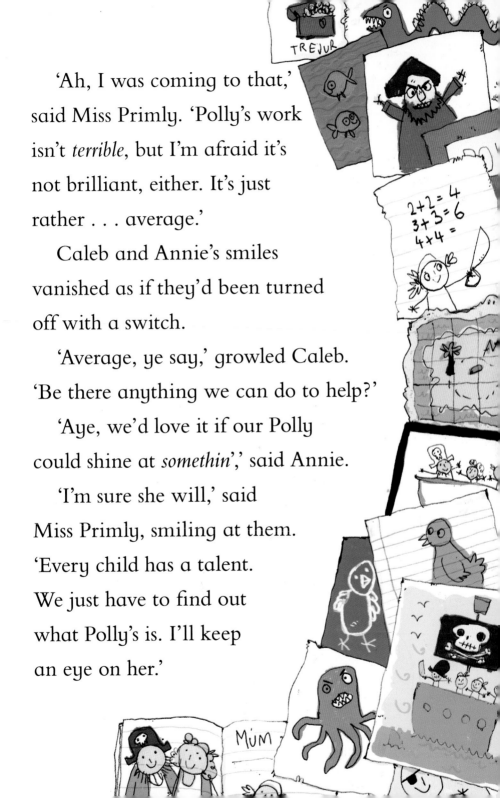

'Ah, I was coming to that,' said Miss Primly. 'Polly's work isn't *terrible*, but I'm afraid it's not brilliant, either. It's just rather . . . average.'

Caleb and Annie's smiles vanished as if they'd been turned off with a switch.

'Average, ye say,' growled Caleb. 'Be there anything we can do to help?'

'Aye, we'd love it if our Polly could shine at *somethin'*,' said Annie.

'I'm sure she will,' said Miss Primly, smiling at them. 'Every child has a talent. We just have to find out what Polly's is. I'll keep an eye on her.'

Miss Primly did just that, and discovered that Polly *was* good at some things. She could certainly climb a rope . . .

. . . and she easily won the Treasure Hunt
competition at the school fair . . . But alas, her
school work didn't improve, no matter how
much Miss Primly or Caleb and Annie tried
to help her.

Then one day Miss Primly took her class on
an outing.

Skull and Crossbones

They were going to the seaside, and Polly was *incredibly* excited.

'Miss Primly says we have to take a packed lunch and a raincoat *and* suncream,' she said. 'Miss Primly says we have to be on our best behaviour at all times. And Miss Primly says we need some parent helpers to come along . . .'

So Caleb and Annie and some of the other parents set off in the coach with Miss Primly and the children.

When they arrived,
they visited the
Sea Life Centre . . .

. . . an interesting
local museum . . .

. . . and ate their lunch
on the beach.

Then for a special treat they went for a boat trip round the harbour.

'Ah, 'tis grand to be back at sea,' said Caleb, taking a deep breath.

'Aye, so it is,' said Annie. 'What about it, Polly – enjoyin' the day?'

'Yes, Ma, it's *brilliant*!' said Polly. 'But hang on . . . what's that?'

Another ship had appeared in the
harbour – a ship bristling with guns, its
crew yelling and waving cutlasses. A ship
flying the skull and crossbones...

'I don't believe it . . .' muttered Caleb.
'It's *The Jolly Herbert*!'

'They be headin' straight for us!' said
Annie. 'Brace yerselves!'

'Prepare to be boarded!' yelled Bad Bart, and the crew of *The Jolly Herbert* swarmed over the side of the harbour boat. Caleb and Annie tried to hold them off, and Miss Primly put up quite a fight, but it was all over pretty quickly.

'Where's Polly?' Annie whispered to Caleb as they were being tied up.

'Wish I knew,' Caleb whispered back. 'Slipped away to hide, maybe . . .'

'Stop that there whispering!' roared Bad Bart. 'Why, if it ain't old Caleb and Annie! Good to see the pair of 'ee . . . er, *not*! And this time ye can join in all the fun! Let's make 'em walk the plank!'

'You can't do that, you nasty, horrible man!' said Miss Primly.

'Shiver me timbers,' roared Bad Bart. 'I'm Bad Bart, the boldest buccaneer on the briny, and I can do whatever I want! Get her on a plank as well, lads!'

'Avast there!' a voice said suddenly. 'Step *away* from the teacher!'

Everyone stopped and looked round at a shadowy, menacing figure.

'And who be ye, then?' said Bad Bart.

The figure stepped forward.

'Me?' she said with a grin. 'I be your worst nightmare.'

Caleb and Annie couldn't believe their eyes.

POLLY!

A Proper Pirate

It *was* Polly, but she looked rather different.
She wasn't wearing her school uniform or her
school shoes any more, and she wasn't carrying
her school bag. Instead she was dressed as a
pirate from top to toe, and she carried a cutlass.

'Don't make me laugh!' growled Bad Bart.
'Ye be just a little girl!'

'Ah, that's what I might look like on the
outside,' said Polly. 'But inside I'm a pirate!
Sorry, Ma and Pa. I've been meanin' to tell
'ee, I've finally realised that this is what I was
born to be!'

With that, Polly grabbed a
rope and swung into the attack.
She knocked over the crew of
The Jolly Herbert like they
were a row of skittles.
Then she chased Bad
Bart back on to *The Jolly
Herbert*, although he
wasn't so easily beaten.
'Lay on with that
there cutlass of yours
and see what it gets 'ee!'
he yelled. 'No quarter,
that's what! I'll send 'ee down
to Davy Jones's locker yet . . .'
Soon Polly and Bad Bart were having a
terrific duel. They charged all over *The Jolly
Herbert*, from the poop deck to the top of a
mast and back again.

'Shiver me timbers, shouldn't we be helping her?' said Caleb.

'No,' laughed Annie. 'She be doin' fine all by herself!'

'By golly, you're right!' said Miss Primly, her voice full of admiration. 'I do believe we've discovered what your daughter's talent is. Go for it, Polly!'

Moments later Bad Bart was on his knees, begging for mercy.

'Three cheers for our piratical Polly!' yelled her Pa. 'Hip, hip . . . hooray!'

That's the end of the story, except to say that Polly went on to be the greatest pirate of all time. Caleb and Annie sailed with their daughter as often as they could, of course, but they also started a business with a new partner.

Teaching at *Miss Primly's Pirate Academy* was a terrific way to pass on everything they had learned. Miss Primly learned a few things too.

As for Bad Bart, well, Caleb and Annie kept him very busy . . . with their new baby.

'Stop that snivellin', Bart!' yelled Annie. 'Just get that nappy changed!'

'Who knows?' said Caleb. 'Ye might even find ye have a talent for it . . .'

The look on Bart's face made them laugh till they cried.

Contents

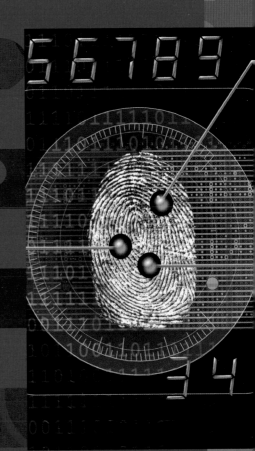

science museum

So you want to solve crimes for a living?

Helping to catch criminals sounds like an incredibly exciting job - and it often is. But being a criminal investigator isn't all about arrests and high-speed car chases.
Real crime detection is a complex business that involves a lot of behind-the-scenes work and research.

Looking at the evidence

In films and TV programmes you will probably have watched villains being caught because of one tiny piece of **evidence** - perhaps a hair or a fingerprint left at the crime scene. When a serious crime is committed, all the evidence at the scene must be looked at very closely, as it could be crucial to solving the case. If specialist knowledge is needed, such as fingerprint or hair analysis, a criminal investigator called a **forensic scientist** does the job.

What is a forensic scientist?

Forensic scientists use science to help answer legal questions, often concerning crime. The word 'forensic' comes from the Latin word 'forum' and describes anything that is related to the law.

Liam Hendrikse, a senior forensic scientist who has worked in London and Canada, says:

'What I find satisfying about my job is being able to provide the Criminal Justice System with the evidence to convict criminals. Also being able to stand up in court and give effective evidence on technical matters in such a way that a jury will easily understand and make the right decision about a suspect.'

Forensic officers at a crime scene

SEARCHING FOR
CRIMINAL INVESTIGATORS!

Are you:

- Interested in science?
- Good at communicating and able to explain things clearly?
- Patient and determined, with an eye for detail?
- Good at concentrating?
- Interested in solving crimes?

Then you might just have what it takes to become a **forensic scientist.**

Forensic fact

TV shows and films that feature crimes and mysteries are not always accurate when it comes to real life. For example, important lab reports seem to be produced almost instantly on TV, when it might take a real forensic scientist many weeks or months to make such an investigation.

What kind of investigator?

There are many different areas that forensic scientists can specialize in, all of them vitally important to the job of catching criminals.

Training

If you want to be a forensic investigator, it is most important to be hardworking and interested in science – most forensics have completed a three- or four-year university **degree** in a science subject, such as chemistry. If successful, you could then go on to study for a postgraduate qualification in forensic science or you might get work as a trainee scientist for an organization that provides forensic services.

Nowadays, some universities offer degree courses that specialize in forensic science right from the start. You'll be attending lectures and laboratory classes in subjects such as chemistry, human biology and legal affairs.

Here are just some of the forensic specialists who help to solve crimes:

- **Trace-evidence examiner**
  Examines anything retrieved from the crime scene that could be used as evidence in court, e.g. hair, glass, fibres from clothes.

- **Firearms/ballistics examiner**
  Identifies bullets and guns to find out where they came from and exactly how they were used in the crime.

- **Forensic pathologist**
  Examines bodies to find out how they died. This examination is called an autopsy.

- **Print examiner**
  Checks any finger-, palm- or footprints left at the crime scene to try to match them to prints on a computer database or prints taken from the suspect.

- **Forensic linguist**
  A language expert who analyses spoken language and text, e.g. confessions, taped conversations, ransom notes.

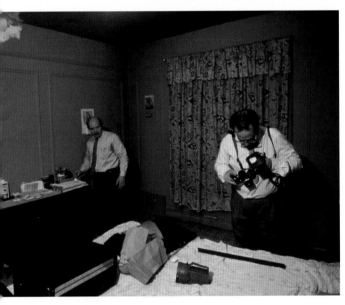

A murder scene

First on the scene

There are many jobs that need to be done before the forensic scientists can begin their work. The police will usually be the first at the scene of a crime, interviewing witnesses and possible suspects and making arrests if necessary. A crime scene photographer may then be called in. Photographs are very important as they are often used as evidence in court and they provide a detailed record of the scene long after everything has been cleared up.

Forensic fact

Anything taken from the crime scene to be examined by forensic scientists needs to be handled very carefully. As people can be identified from microscopic traces of evidence, it is vitally important that nothing is contaminated by the investigator, who wears a special polypropylene (plastic) suit and surgical gloves. All potential evidence is carefully packed into sealed containers and labelled.

Forensics in history

Forensic science sounds like a very modern subject, but in fact the roots of today's advanced investigations go back hundreds of years.

Prints of the past

- It seems that humans have always been interested in **fingerprints**. Impressions of fingers have been found in prehistoric rock carvings and in clay tablets from ancient China and Arabia.

- The earliest known use of fingerprints for identification was in **seventh-century Arabia**, where the fingerprints of debtors – people who borrowed money from a lender – were made on the lender's bill as proof of the debt.

- An Italian called **Malpighi** studied fingerprints in 1686 and noted their distinctive patterns, but it wasn't until 1892 that a man called **Francis Galton** came up with a method of classifying fingerprints so that they could be used to identify criminals. The fingerprint system became widely used by the police just a few years later.

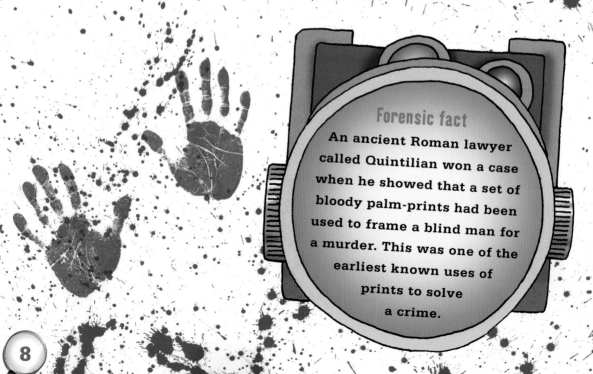

Forensic fact

An ancient Roman lawyer called Quintilian won a case when he showed that a set of bloody palm-prints had been used to frame a blind man for a murder. This was one of the earliest known uses of prints to solve a crime.

The forensic fly

In the past, the usual way of finding someone guilty of a crime was to make them confess, or to find an **eyewitness** - someone who actually saw what had happened. Science was not considered. There is only one early account of a scientific method being used to solve a crime, from China in 1248. It describes how a man was murdered with a sickle (a blade used for cutting crops). The investigator ordered everyone who had been at the scene to bring their sickles to him. Then he waited. Flies eventually gathered on one sickle, attracted by the smell of blood - the blood itself had been washed off - and the murderer confessed to his crime.

CRACKING THE CASE

- In sixteenth-century Europe, people began gathering proper information and evidence that could be used to solve crimes. Members of the medical profession started to study the cause and manner of deaths. This was the beginning of modern pathology.

- The first use of physical evidence to convict a man is believed to have taken place in 1784, when an Englishman called John Toms was accused of murdering a man with a pistol. Toms was convicted when a torn piece of newspaper that was stuffed inside the pistol was found to fit together with a piece of newspaper in his pocket.

- Many other advances were made throughout the nineteenth and twentieth centuries, in areas such as microscopy and toxicology (the study of poisons). A huge amount of knowledge was gained, and modern forensic science was born.

Amazing advances

Crimes have been committed throughout history – it's just our ways of solving them that have changed. In the last hundred years, important scientific breakthroughs have meant that criminals who might have walked free in the past have now been convicted.

The right person?

As well as fingerprinting, other new ways of identifying suspects have been developed, such as:

- **Identikit** – a system of 'building' a face from eyewitness accounts.
- **Anthropometry** – using body measurements to help identification.
- **Computer simulation programs** that can visualize human faces.
- **The DNA profiling test** (see page 19)

'Seeing' the evidence

The invention of powerful new **precision microscopes** has enabled investigators to look at evidence more closely. For instance, the phase-contrast microscope, built in 1938, made it possible to observe individual cells. Advances in the use of ultraviolet light have revealed evidence such as saliva, hairs, fibres and prints which could not be seen under normal lighting.

Bodily matters

The invention of X-rays and new methods of testing blood – including the 1901 discovery that human blood can be classified into different groups – have helped investigators to identify suspects and find out more about causes of death. The discovery that **human hair** can be used as evidence has helped in many investigations.

EXHIBIT 'A'

10

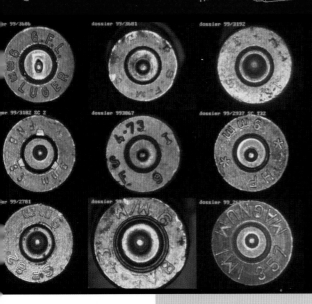

Forensic database
of bullet casings

Know your weapon

Methods of matching bullets to guns have been invented and refined, and new tests were developed to find gunshot residue (see page 22). In 1920 an international catalogue of firearms was begun. This has enabled many guns to be identified.

FORENSIC FIRSTS

Each of these cases was solved by a new scientific method used for the first time:

1898

Bullet breakthrough

A German chemist solves a murder case by taking the suspect's gun and firing a bullet from it. The markings on the bullet are shown to match those on a bullet found earlier at the murder scene. This evidence is used to convict the suspect.

1902

Print power

Henry Jackson's fingerprints are used to convict him of burglary – the first time fingerprint evidence has been used in an English court.

1926

Microscopic markings

The invention of the comparison microscope (see page 17) enables investigators to see tiny markings on bullets fired at the crime scene. Two killers are sent to jail.

1986

Chemical conviction

The first time that DNA profiling is used to identify and convict a murderer. During this case DNA profiling was also used to prove that another suspect was innocent.

Forensic fact

A police inspector called Edmond Locard once said that 'Every contact leaves a trace' – meaning that criminals cannot prevent leaving traces of themselves at a crime scene. This phrase has since formed the basis of forensic science.

Examining the crime scene

Wherever a serious crime has taken place, a team of skilled people will soon be on the scene. They know that any evidence found here could be the key to solving the case.

First on the scene

The **scene-of-crime team**, headed by a senior investigating officer, arrives and the crime scene is sealed off with tape. From now on, only authorized people can enter the area – the fewer visitors, the better. Too many stray hairs and shoeprints will make the job of collecting evidence more difficult.

The **senior officer** will take detailed notes and may record a description of the scene on a hand-held tape recorder.

A **crime photographer** takes photos and often makes a video of the scene from different angles as well as close-ups of relevant objects. Sketches (reconstructions) may also be made to show where everything is. Every crime is different so each search is tailored towards the type and nature of the crime.

The Murder Scene

IF A CAR OR OTHER VEHICLE HAS BEEN USED, PRINTS FROM TYRES MAY BE FOUND OUTSIDE.

IF A FIREARM HAS BEEN USED, THERE MAY BE BULLET HOLES OR CASINGS AROUND.

Crime-scene reconstruction

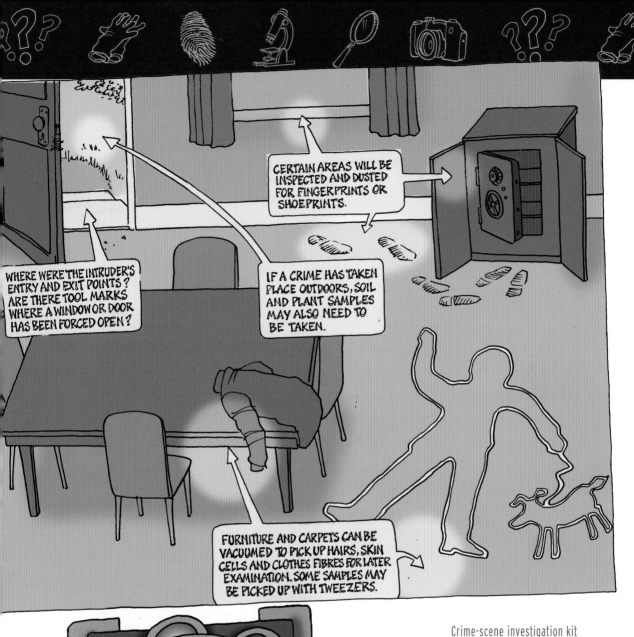

CERTAIN AREAS WILL BE INSPECTED AND DUSTED FOR FINGERPRINTS OR SHOEPRINTS.

WHERE WERE THE INTRUDER'S ENTRY AND EXIT POINTS? ARE THERE TOOL MARKS WHERE A WINDOW OR DOOR HAS BEEN FORCED OPEN?

IF A CRIME HAS TAKEN PLACE OUTDOORS, SOIL AND PLANT SAMPLES MAY ALSO NEED TO BE TAKEN.

FURNITURE AND CARPETS CAN BE VACUUMED TO PICK UP HAIRS, SKIN CELLS AND CLOTHES FIBRES FOR LATER EXAMINATION. SOME SAMPLES MAY BE PICKED UP WITH TWEEZERS.

Forensic fact

The crime photographer uses **scale tape** to measure a piece of evidence. This will show everyone in court the true size of the object in question, as it is very difficult to tell from a photograph how large or small something is.

Crime-scene investigation kit

Fingerprinting is still one of the most accurate methods that forensic science can use to identify people.

Fingerprint facts

- Every person's fingerprints are different – even those of identical twins.
- Fingerprints are formed before you are born and they stay the same throughout your life.
- Fingerprints are nature's way of making sure we can hold on to things. Without those tiny ridges of flesh under your skin you would have great difficulty turning the pages of this book.

It's all in the prints

It's incredible to think that every one of the many millions of people in the world has a completely unique pattern of curves and loops on their fingertips. Fingerprint experts classify these patterns into ten groups. The most common of these are:

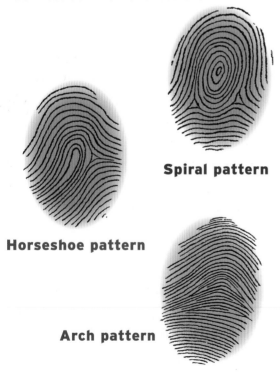

Spiral pattern

Horseshoe pattern

Arch pattern

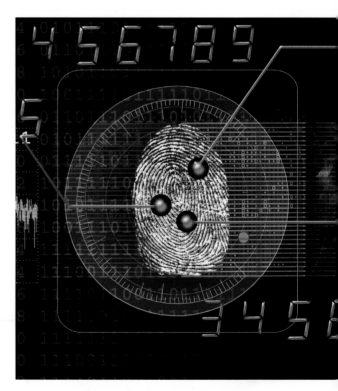

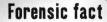

Forensic fact

The largest collection of fingerprints in existence is held by the Federal Bureau of Investigation (FBI) in the United States. It contains over 250 million sets of prints.

How to find a fingerprint

When a hand touches a smooth surface, the oil in the skin leaves behind an impression of the finger's pattern. If the print is clear, you can take a photograph or 'lift' the print by laying low-adhesive transparent tape over it to carefully lift off the pattern. However, prints cannot always be seen by the human eye so other **detection methods** are needed:

- Use coloured fingerprint powder and a soft brush to dust all over the surface and reveal the print.
- Even if the criminal has been careful not to leave any prints behind, look out for 'partials' – just a tiny part of a fingerprint.
- On some surfaces you will need to use special chemicals and lighting to see the prints. One method is to use the moist fumes from superglue, which helps make some prints visible. Ultraviolet light or lasers can then be used to illuminate the print even more.

A fingerprint expert in 1938

A skilful eye

A trained **forensic print examiner** can compare the print with the many thousands that are stored in a police computer database. Even though there is a special computer programme that can match prints, the final decision is down to the fingerprint expert, who may spend days analysing a tiny 'partial' print. The job takes a great deal of skill and concentration.

The prints on the database belong to people who have been arrested on suspicion of committing a crime. They are taken by rolling the fingers on to an ink pad. The prints are then scanned electronically (digitized). Alternatively, the fingerprints can be electronically scanned straight into the computer.

Tell-tale traces

It isn't just fingerprints that criminals may leave behind them. There may be 'trace evidence' for the forensic team to investigate.

Shoeprints and tyre tracks

Both shoes and tyres have distinctive patterns on their soles and treads, which can be used to link a suspect to a crime. Getting a clear enough print depends on the type of ground the print was made on and how deep the impression is.

Get the impression

- **Clear prints** may be photographed or filled with plaster to make a cast. Even footprints made in snow can be cast if the print is first sprayed with hairspray.
- Prints made in **dust** are more difficult to retrieve, but they can be lifted using a special layer of sticky gel on a piece of fabric.
- Another method is to use an **Electrostatic Lifting Machine** (ELM), which passes an electric current through a dusty print so that it is lifted on to a piece of black foil.

Tread carefully

Just as with fingerprinting, the forensic expert can try to match a shoe- or tyre-print with one of the many patterns held on a database. Footwear companies help by supplying the patterns of their shoe treads, and there are also databases of shoeprints taken from known criminals. Similarly, tyre-tread databases can help identify types of vehicle. Marks from wear and tear are helpful as they are unique to the shoe or tyre.

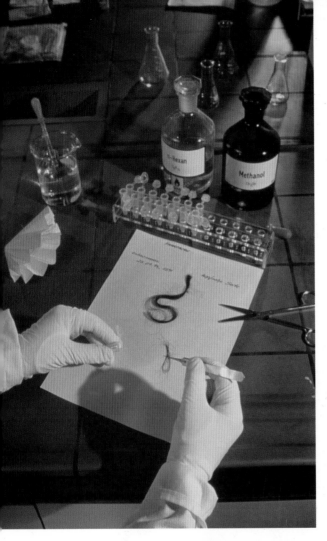

Helpful hair

The forensic scientist can use a **single hair** for identification in various ways. A chemical called DNA (see pages 18-19) can be extracted from the hair or it can be analysed for trace metals. Everyone's hair contains tiny amounts of metals, such as copper and gold, and the combination is unique to each person. A comparison microscope can be used to compare hair colour, traces of hair dye and even signs of disease.

The comparison microscope

This nifty piece of equipment is essential for the forensic investigator.

It is basically a combination of two microscopes that enables someone to observe any two samples at the same time, under the same lighting. It is needed to compare and match tiny samples such as hairs, fragments and fibres.

Testing hair sample in a forensic laboratory

Forensic fact

Caught by a holey sock! A thief in Scotland wore gloves while burgling houses to prevent his fingerprints being left behind. However, on one occasion, he removed his shoes — and left a toe-print behind through a hole in his sock. He was identified and caught.

Dynamic DNA

A single hair or a speck of blood is all that the forensic scientist now needs to identify a suspect or prove a person's innocence. DNA fingerprinting is probably the most exciting breakthrough ever made in forensic science.

Human traces

Tiny particles from the human body are often left behind when a crime is committed. Burglars may cut themselves on glass when they climb through a window; criminals might leave saliva on a piece of chewing gum or drops of perspiration might contain microscopic skin cells. Traces like these contain vital human evidence called **DNA**.

What is DNA?

DNA stands for **deoxyribo-nucleic acid**, a chemical that is found in almost every cell in our bodies. DNA carries genetic information that is passed down through our families, giving us our physical characteristics such as height, eye colour and skin colour. Every person's DNA is completely unique (apart from identical twins). Scientists can extract DNA from many parts of the body, including blood, skin cells, saliva and hair.

Model of the double-helix DNA molecule

How to take a DNA 'fingerprint'

Obtaining a DNA 'fingerprint' is far more complicated than taking a regular fingerprint.

Firstly the forensic scientist must extract enough DNA from the cell sample to do the test. The microscopic fragments of DNA are then sorted in a complex electrical process. The fragments are arranged into groups and coloured with different fluorescent dyes for identification.

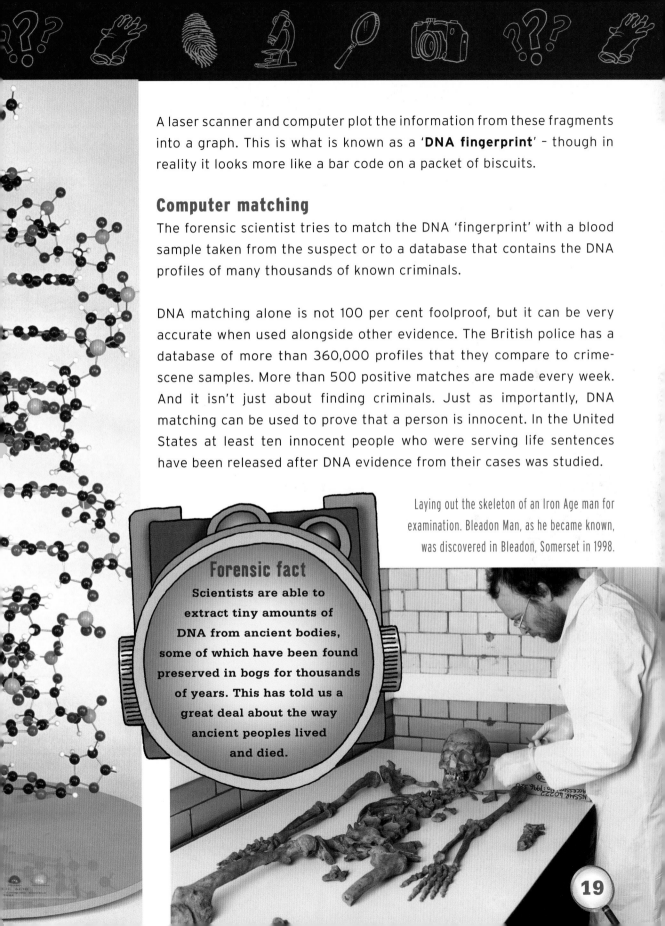

A laser scanner and computer plot the information from these fragments into a graph. This is what is known as a '**DNA fingerprint**' – though in reality it looks more like a bar code on a packet of biscuits.

Computer matching

The forensic scientist tries to match the DNA 'fingerprint' with a blood sample taken from the suspect or to a database that contains the DNA profiles of many thousands of known criminals.

DNA matching alone is not 100 per cent foolproof, but it can be very accurate when used alongside other evidence. The British police has a database of more than 360,000 profiles that they compare to crime-scene samples. More than 500 positive matches are made every week. And it isn't just about finding criminals. Just as importantly, DNA matching can be used to prove that a person is innocent. In the United States at least ten innocent people who were serving life sentences have been released after DNA evidence from their cases was studied.

Laying out the skeleton of an Iron Age man for examination. Bleadon Man, as he became known, was discovered in Bleadon, Somerset in 1998.

Forensic fact
Scientists are able to extract tiny amounts of DNA from ancient bodies, some of which have been found preserved in bogs for thousands of years. This has told us a great deal about the way ancient peoples lived and died.

Identifying a body

Dealing with dead people is not for everyone, but several kinds of forensic investigator do this work. If an unidentified body is found, their skills are needed to solve the mystery.

SKULL

In the bones

A **forensic pathologist**, who is also a trained doctor, has the job of examining bodies to find the cause of death. But if a person has been dead for a long time there may only be a skeleton or a few bones left to examine. Putting together a picture of the person takes great skill and, in some cases, artistic talent.

The bone detective

A **forensic anthropologist** is an expert on human growth and development. He or she can piece together bones, rather like a jigsaw puzzle, to work out whether the person was a man or woman and to estimate their age, weight and height. Bones can give us amazing insights into people's lives – they can even tell us what kind of jobs people once did. For example, a bony ridge that has developed on the wrist is a sign that someone used their hands a lot in their job and could perhaps have worked as a cook or a dressmaker.

Bleadon Man's skull. He had developed a robust jawbone because his food had contained a lot of grit.

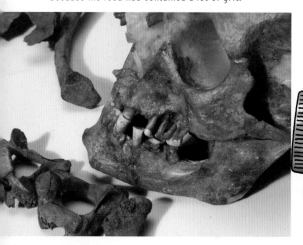

Forensic fact

The teeth are the hardest part of the body and may be the last parts remaining of a very old corpse. A **forensic odontologist** is an expert in identifying and analysing teeth.

- Measuring the **skull** gives us information about age and racial background.

- If there is any **hair tissue**, DNA may be extracted for identification.

- The condition of the **teeth** can tell us a lot about the health, age and lifestyle of a person. Teeth can also be matched up to dental records and X-rays for identification, and are also used for DNA extraction.

- Looking at the place where the ribs join the **sternum** is a good way of estimating age. For instance, the ends of the ribs are usually flatter in young people.

- Trying to wiggle a thumb in the notch of the **pelvis** can reveal the sex of the person. Women have wider pelvises and there will be room to wiggle the thumb, unlike in men.

TEETH

STERNUM

PELVIS

WRIST

The forensic sculptor

If you are talented at both art and science, this might be the job for you.

Forensic sculptors make three-dimensional models, usually from clay, of people's heads and faces, to try to give an idea of what a person once looked like. Reconstructing a face is a very skilled and painstaking procedure and sometimes you may only have a line drawing to work from. Every muscle and piece of tissue that lies under the skin needs to be gradually built up to produce a realistic facial structure. Eyeballs and skin are the final touches to create a lifelike face.

Lethal weapons

If a gun is fired, investigators will do everything possible to find the person who pulled the trigger. They know that using a firearm can leave behind important clues.

What happened?

Arriving at the crime scene, the forensic team will first try to find out how many bullets were fired. Witnesses may be able to tell them the number of shots that were fired or, if the weapon has been left behind, the forensic investigator may be able to work this out from the number of unfired bullets left in the gun. They will then search for:

- the **bullet**(s) used
- the **cartridge**(s) – the case around the bullet
- any traces of **powder** that flew out as the bullet left the gun.

Finding this evidence helps the firearms forensic work out each bullet's **trajectory** – the path of the bullet from when it was fired to where it ended up. The crime may then be reconstructed, giving details such as where the criminal was standing and the kind of weapon that was used.

In the lab

Any bullets or cartridge cases are taken back to the lab for closer inspection. Markings on a cartridge case can tell the investigator a lot about the weapon that fired it, e.g. the mechanism of a particular gun may scratch the cartridge in a unique way when it is fired. Finding and linking the gun to its owner is the next step. Tiny amounts of powder residue are often found not only around a gunshot wound but also on the hands, clothes or face of the person who pulled the trigger. All suspects are tested for this residue, which is then compared to that found at the scene.

Policeman firing a pistol retrieved from a crime scene at a paper target in order to identify the bullet patterns

A day in the life of a firearms forensic

Liam Hendrikse is a senior forensic scientist who specializes in firearms. He studied for a chemistry degree, then a Masters in Forensic Science, followed by several years of training at the **Forensic Science Service** (FSS) in London. The FSS works with the police force to solve crimes in the UK.

'My day starts with casework duties, examining guns and ammunition, test-firing guns in a special range and writing statements for use in court, where I sometimes have to appear to give evidence as an expert witness. On some days I am called out to the crime scene to help reconstruct the sequence of events and to identify the types of weapon used. When I'm working in the lab, I try to link crimes by using a comparison microscope to examine fired bullets and cartridge cases.'

Forensic fact

In 1835 Scotland Yard's Henry Goddard first used bullet comparison to solve a murder case. He found a flaw in the bullet and traced it back to its original mould, providing the link that was needed to catch the killer.

23

Fakes and Forgeries

How do we know if a painting or a document is the 'real thing' - or simply a fake? Specialist forensic investigators can find out.

Authentic art?

Many paintings have been forged throughout history – copies made of the most famous painting in the world, the *Mona Lisa*, have fooled many experts in the past. It isn't always easy to tell if a painting is the real thing but forensic investigators have scientific methods of detecting forgeries, such as:

- **Looking at the material the painting has been made on.** If it is painted on wood, the type and age of wood can point us towards the period in history when the painting was made. Canvas can also be examined to see what it is made from and the type of weave that was popular at the time, e.g. cotton canvases only came into use after cotton was commercially produced in the nineteenth century.

- **Analysing the type of paint used.** Older paints were often made from materials that were only used at a certain time in history. One forger was recently discovered because he painted his fakes with modern household emulsion (used for painting walls), something that certainly wasn't used by artists of the past!

- **Microscopic examination** can reveal whether the cracked, ageing look of paint is real or simulated.

- **Infrared scanning and X-rays** reveal details that can't be seen in normal light – there may be another painting underneath or alterations may have been made that show the painting is not authentic.

The document detective

There are lots of reasons why criminals might want to alter or forge an important document. Changing the terms of a will, forging passports and altering important contracts are just some of them.

Questions a forensic handwriting expert would ask:

Is the handwriting authentic?

No two people have the same writing. A **handwriting expert** can compare the shapes and style of two pieces of writing to say whether they are by the same person. Some people believe that handwriting is as identifiable as fingerprints.

Has the document been altered?

Somebody may have added extra text or deleted some text to replace it with new wording. The ink that has been used can be analysed in a process called **spectroscopy** to see if any words have been written using a different pen. There is also a system called **video-imaging spectral analysis**, which can highlight alterations and additions made to documents. This can even tell the expert if a signature was made on a document before or after the document was filled out.

Has the document been tampered with?

Close examination may reveal that pages have been taken out of or added into a long document such as a will.

What equipment has been used?

Forensic investigators can check to see which kind of machine produced a document – typewriter, photocopier, fax machine or PC. They may also be able to identify the exact machine that produced it.

Forensic fact

Two men were convicted of murder in the USA in 1924 when forensic investigators showed that a typewriter belonging to one of the men had been used to type the ransom note.

25

Computer criminals

It is hard to imagine a world without computers. Their existence has transformed our lives in many ways – but they have also transformed the way criminals operate.

The computer forensic expert

This type of investigator is trained to search computers and other devices – fax machines, MP3 players and mobile phones, for example – to retrieve information that could help with the investigation. He or she will dismantle and study any hardware seized by police, identifying and photographing each part before analysing the data. This data could be vital information that makes or breaks a case. Dates and times of meetings, suspicious emails – these could be used as evidence in court. The computer forensic expert has the skills and the software to root out deleted data and emails and stolen data, as well as hidden files and folders.

What is computer crime?

Most computer crime falls into one of these groups:

1. **Hacking** – a 'hacker' is someone who 'breaks in' to a computer or network without the owner's permission. He or she may want to obtain secret information or just prove that it can be done.

2. **Computer fraud** – this covers a number of different crimes, from manipulating computerized banking systems in order to steal money to making illegal credit-card transactions.

3. **Piracy** – computer software is illegally copied and sold. The creators of the software lose out on their rightful income.

4. **Computer viruses** – creating programs that contain viruses and sending them out to disable people's computers and software.

History of a hacker

In the early 1980s a computer-crazy teenager called **Kevin Mitnick** managed to break into the high-security North American Air Defense terminal (providing the idea for the 1983 film *War Games*). He later became one of the most infamous computer hackers in the word.

He broke into company systems, causing great damage and expense, and accessed the private financial information of hundreds of people. After a spell in prison Mitnick was released, but he continued his illegal activities. He was eventually tracked down by a top computer-security expert working with the FBI. They used a specially designed computer program to monitor a database that they believed Mitnick was accessing. He was caught and served another jail sentence.

Forensic fact

A woman in the UK recently became the first victim of a computer 'kidnapping' when she discovered that her computer files had vanished, replaced by a mysterious folder entitled 'How to get your files back'. A computer forensic expert managed to recover some of her files, but the criminals have not yet been located.

27

The future for forensics

As a forensic scientist you will already be using the latest developments in science and technology. But there's more to come.

Instant images

DNA fingerprinting was an amazing discovery, but the technology just gets better all the time. Until now, a typical DNA 'fingerprint' has needed 200–500 human cells for an effective result. Soon, just a **single cell** will be enough to build a profile. And that profile will allow us to see a **3D image** of the suspect, complete with hair and eye colour, height and skin type. It may even be able to tell us about the person's personality!

Scientists also believe that, in the near future, the complex process of DNA fingerprinting could take just minutes. Police will be supplied with **hi-tech hand-held devices** that can 'decode' DNA at the crime scene – so there will be no need to send samples off to the lab and wait for the results.

Forensic scientists preparing blood-stained clothing (jeans, a T-shirt and a shoe) and an axe for blood sampling

Forensic fact

DNA fingerprinting was accidentally discovered by Professor Alec Jeffreys in 1984 during a research project that involved the extraction of DNA from blood. He found a way to measure the lengths of microscopic fragments of DNA using radioactive probing, producing an X-ray of the results in the form of a 'barcode'. It was an incredibly exciting moment.

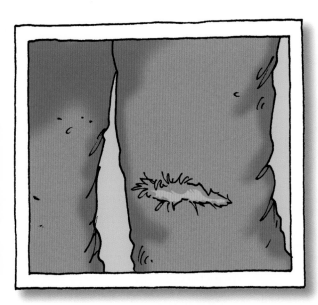

It's all in the detail

Closed Circuit Television (CCTV) has helped investigators to identify criminals many times in the past. But forget about fuzzy headshots and blurred body images. The way ahead is **Digital Image Enhancement**, a programme that can make the fuzziest picture recognizable. The technology is now at the stage where it can do a close up on, for example, a pair of jeans worn by the suspect, scanning every wrinkle, seam and mark. This 'image map' can be digitized and held on a database where it might later be matched up to a pair found in the suspect's wardrobe.

Having a brainwave

Could we one day actually be able to 'see' inside a suspect's brain to find out if they are innocent or guilty? This futuristic idea is already in development. In 1999 Dr Lawrence Farwell developed the controversial technique he called **Brain Fingerprinting**, a computer-based method of measuring brainwaves. It works by showing a suspect details of their alleged crime on a screen. Their brain activity is measured as they watch, and Farwell claims that if their brain recognizes the crime, the computer detects a particular brainwave response. The technology has been used in cases in the USA, where suspects have volunteered to take the test in order to prove their innocence.

29

From crime lab to court case

Whichever kind of investigator you want to be, you will need scientific skills plus the ability to communicate with people. Presenting your work in court is a vital part of the job.

Location, location, location

As a forensic investigator you will be working in several different but equally important places. Much of your time will be spent in the **laboratory**, where you will be carrying out your scientific investigations. Some of your time could be spent investigating the actual crime scene. On other days you will be asked to attend **court**, to present and explain your findings.

In the crime lab

The laboratories where forensic scientists work are modern buildings containing all the hi-tech equipment needed for investigations, from supplies of chemicals and hi-intensity ultraviolet lamps to the latest comparison microscopes and scanners. All the evidence from the crime scene is brought here for analysis.

At court

Appearing in court is a very different experience. You will be expected to present your report as a written document and you may also have to answer questions from the legal teams. Forensic experts must be able to explain technical and scientific information in a way that ordinary people will understand. In criminal courts, you may be asked to appear for either the prosecution or the defence. You may also be asked to give evidence in civil cases, for example, providing information about the cause of a road accident or a fire.

Forensic fact

Forensic scientists in DNA testing labs have to be very careful not to transfer microscopic traces of DNA from one place to another, as this could affect test results. They wear sterile masks, gloves and coats and they work in specially air-conditioned labs that have air sucked out of them (rather than blown in) if the door is opened. This reduces the risk of contamination.

Forensics – is it for you?

Being a forensic investigator is not like any other job. The unique combination of science and criminal investigation has an incredibly important role to play in the courts. Your forensic report may be used to help send a guilty person to prison – or, just as importantly, to prove that someone is innocent and set them free. Being a forensic investigator must surely be one of the most fascinating and satisfying jobs around.

At The Science Museum you can entertain people of any age with **exhibitions**, events, **films**, **food** and shops – all under one roof, for anything from an hour to a day.

science museum

Entry to the Museum is FREE, but charges apply to our IMAX cinema, simulators and special exhibitions. Family, discounted and combination tickets available. Call **0870 870 4846** for more information.

Science Museum, Exhibition Road, London SW7 2DD **www.sciencemuseum.org.uk**

Macmillan Children's Books is delighted to be publishing the following brilliant books in association with The Science Museum.

WOW – Discoveries
that changed the world
Philip Ardagh
978-0-330-44453-8
£3.99

WOW – Inventions
that changed the world
Philip Ardagh
978-0-330-44454-5
£3.99

WOW - Ideas
that changed the world
Philip Ardagh
978-0-330-44875-8
£3.99

WOW - Events
that changed the world
Philip Ardagh
978-0-330-44874-1
£3.99

Aliens – are we alone?
Amanda Li
978-0-330-44118-6
£3.99

Why is Snot Green?
Glenn Murphy
978-0-330-44852-9
£4.99

How to Be an
Astronaut
Amanda Li
978-0-330-44614-3
£3.99

How to Be a
Brain Surgeon
Amanda Li
978-0-330-44615-0
£3.99

How to Be a
Vet
Amanda Li
978-0-230-01543-2
£3.99

The Science Museum
Activity Book
978-0-330-44550-4
£2.99

The Science Museum
Sticker Activity Book
978-0-330-44784-3
£3.99

All **Pan Macmillan** titles can be bought from our website, **www.panmacmillan.com**, from the Science Museum Shop or your local bookshop.

They are also available by post from: **Bookpost**, PO Box 29, Douglas, Isle of Man IM99 1BQ. Credit cards accepted.
For details: telephone: 01624 677237, fax: 01624 670923, email: bookshop@enterprise.net, **www.bookpost.co.uk**
Free postage and packing in the United Kingdom.